SOMETHING BAD

Raising his hand to knock on the door, Ricky realized that Robin might also hear, so instead, he clutched the doorknob and slowly turned it. As the door swung silently inward, he heard the steady whirring of the ceiling fans within the room.

"Mom?" he whispered. "Dad?"

They didn't wake up, so h̶e̶ ̶s̶t̶e̶p̶p̶ed inside, closing the door behind him.

"Mom?" he called ̶.̶.̶.̶ louder. "Mom?"

He approached ̶.̶.̶.̶ ring against his rib cage. Altho̶.̶.̶.̶ n and the cool northerly b̶.̶.̶.̶nts' bedroom, hot and clo̶.̶.̶.̶t smell that made the hairs o̶.̶.̶.̶ckle up.

He ste̶.̶.̶.̶d, thinking that it was strange that his par̶.̶.̶.̶r their quilt on such a hot night. He reached ̶.̶.̶.̶tapped the quilt, about where his mother's should̶.̶.̶. should be.

She didn't wake up.

"Mom?" he asked, poking at the quilt a little harder.

The material felt funny, sticky-damp.

"Dad!" Leaning across her, he shook his father. "Dad!"

Suddenly he lost his tiptoed balance and fell on them, landing facedown, mouth open, on the quilt. Abruptly he became aware that the sticky dampness was everywhere, and as he breathed in its rusty metal smell, he realized it was in his mouth, and he recognized the flavor of blood. . . .

Books by Tamara Thorne

HAUNTED

MOONFALL

ETERNITY

CANDLE BAY

BAD THINGS

THE FORGOTTEN

THUNDER ROAD

THE SORORITY

Published by Kensington Publishing Corporation